Written by Sue Graves
Illustrated by Jan Lewis
Designed by Blue Sunflower Creative

Language consultant: Betty Root

This is a Parragon Publishing book
This edition published in 2004

Parragon Publishing
Queen Street House
4 Queen Street
Bath, BA1 1HE, UK

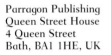

ISBN 1-40541-860-5
Printed in China

Lost in the Jungle

p

Notes for Parents

Reading with your child is an enjoyable and rewarding experience. These **Gold Stars** reading books encourage and support children who are learning to read.

The **Gold Stars** reading books are filled with fun stories, familiar vocabulary, and amusing pictures. Sharing these books with your child will ensure that reading is fun. It is important, at this early stage, for children to enjoy reading and succeed. Success creates confidence.

Starting to read

Start by reading the book aloud to your child, taking time to talk about the pictures. This will help your child to see that pictures often give clues about the story.

Over a period of time, try to read the same book several times so that your child becomes familiar with the story and the words and phrases. Gradually, your child will want to read the book aloud with you. It helps to run your finger under the words as you say them.

Occasionally, stop and encourage your child to continue reading aloud without you. Join in again when your child needs help. This is the next step toward helping your child become an independent reader.

Finally, your child will be ready to read alone. Listen carefully to your child and give plenty of praise. Remember to make reading an enjoyable experience.

Using your Gold Stars stickers

You can use the **Gold Stars** stickers at the back of the book as a reward for effort as well as achievement. Learning to read is an exciting challenge for every child.

Remember these four important stages:

- Read the story **to** your child.
- Read the story **with** your child.
- Encourage your child to read **to you**.
- Listen to your child read **alone**.

Every year, Pete and Poppy went on vacation.

They went on vacation with Uncle Charlie and Aunt Molly.

"This year," said Uncle Charlie, "we are going on a safari."

"What's a safari?" asked Pete.

"A safari is a trip through the jungle," said Aunt Molly.

What's a safari?

Pete and Poppy packed all their vacation items. They took lots and lots of things with them. Poppy took a floppy sun hat.

"This will keep me cool!" she said.

Pete packed a map and a compass.

This will keep me cool!

"You won't need a map and a compass," said Uncle Charlie. "We are going to a special part of the jungle. There are special paths for us to follow."

But Pete still packed his map and compass.

The next day, they went to the jungle.

"This is our camp," said Aunt Molly.

The jungle was hot.

Poppy put on her sun hat to keep her cool.

Pete got out his map and a compass. "We are here," he said. He put a big cross on the map.

"We don't need a map and a compass," said Uncle Charlie. "Everyone follow me!"

They went deep into the jungle. A sign by the path said "To the lake."

"This way," said Uncle Charlie.
Aunt Molly, Poppy, and Pete followed him.

To the lake

Uncle Charlie followed the path through the jungle. Pete followed the path on his map.

"We're going north," said Pete.

"Excellent!" said Uncle Charlie. "Excellent!"

Soon, they came to the lake. Lots of animals were there. Some were drinking; some were washing; and some were playing.

"We mustn't get too close," said Aunt Molly. She took lots of pictures.

Pete looked at his map.

"We are here," he said. He put another big cross on the map.

"We don't need a map and a compass," said Uncle Charlie. "This way!"

They went deeper into the jungle. A sign by the path said "To the lions."

"This way," said Uncle Charlie.
Aunt Molly, Poppy, and Pete followed him.

To camp

To the lions

We're going east now.

Uncle Charlie followed the path
through the jungle. Pete followed the path
on his map.

"We're going east now," he said.

"Excellent!" said Uncle Charlie. "Excellent!"

Soon, they came to the lions. The lions were sleeping under the trees.

"We mustn't get too close," said Aunt Molly. She took lots of pictures.

Pete looked at his map.

"We are here," he said. He put another big cross on his map.

"Time for lunch," said Uncle Charlie. "This way!"

They went deeper into the jungle. A sign by the path said "Picnic Place."

Pete looked at his map.

"We are here," he said. He put another big cross on his map.

Aunt Molly unpacked the lunch. Pete and Poppy ate lots of sandwiches.

"Do not feed the animals," said Uncle Charlie. He ate a large banana.

"Time we went back to camp," said Uncle Charlie. "This way!"

They went back along the path, but the signs were gone.

"Oh, no, the sign has gone," said Aunt Molly.

"We're lost in the jungle!" said Poppy.
"Don't worry," said Pete. "We can follow the
path on my map. We must go back the way
we came. This way!"

Soon, they were back at the camp.

"You were right, Pete," said Uncle Charlie.
"We did need a map and a compass."

Everyone laughed and laughed. Aunt Molly took lots and lots of pictures.

"This vacation has been fun," said Pete. "But can we go to the seashore next year? I think I need a rest."

I think
I need a rest!

Answer these questions. Look back in the book to find the answers.

Who was going on vacation?

What did Pete
take with him?

Where were they going?

Where did they have lunch?

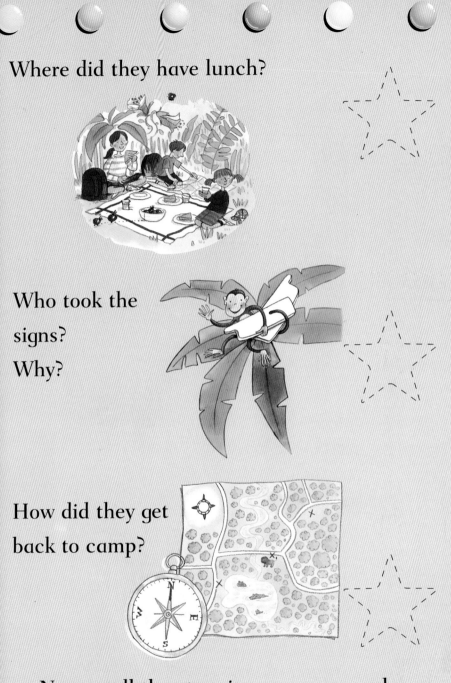

Who took the
signs?
Why?

How did they get
back to camp?

Now retell the story in your own words.

Gold Stars

Gold Stars reading books are for children who are beginning to read.

- Familiar, repeated vocabulary
- Short sentences
- Large, clear type
- Pictures that support the text
- Review activity